Check out Princess Poppy's website
to find out all about the other
books in the series

www.princesspoppy.com

Princess Poppy
The Rescue Princess

Princess Poppy
The Rescue
Princess

written by Janey Louise Jones
Illustrated by Samantha Chaffey

YOUNG CORGI

THE RESCUE PRINCESS
A YOUNG CORGI BOOK 978 0 552 55701 6

Published in Great Britain by Young Corgi,
an imprint of Random House Children's Books
A Random House Group Company

This edition published 2008

3 5 7 9 10 8 6 4 2

Text copyright © Janey Louise Jones, 2008
Illustrations copyright © Random House Children's Books, 2008
Illustrations by Samantha Chaffey

The Random House Group Limited makes every effort to ensure that the
papers used in its books are made from trees that have been legally sourced
from well-managed and credibly certified forests. Our paper procurement
policy can be found at: www.randomhouse.co.uk/paper.htm

Mixed Sources
Product group from well-managed
forests and other controlled sources
www.fsc.org Cert no. TT-COC-2139
© 1996 Forest Stewardship Council

Set in 15/21pt Bembo MT Schoolbook by
Falcon Oast Graphic Art Ltd.

Young Corgi Books are published by Random House Children's Books,
61–63 Uxbridge Road, London W5 5SA,

www.princesspoppy.com
www.rbooks.co.uk

Addresses for companies within The Random House Group Limited can be
found at: www.randomhouse.co.uk/offices.htm

THE RANDOM HOUSE GROUP Limited Reg. No. 954009

A CIP catalogue record for this book is available from the British Library.

Printed in the UK by CPI William Clowes Ltd,
Beccles, NR34 7TL

To Lindsey Fraser, with grateful thanks
for all your help

Chapter One

Poppy loved cosy nights in, especially Fridays. School was over for another week, and when the weather was cold, there was always a roaring fire in the sitting room at Honeysuckle Cottage, which made things seem even cosier. The smell of Mum's home-baked bread and Victoria sponges, both regular weekend treats, wafted in from the kitchen stove. But tonight Poppy was even happier than usual because she was having her first

1

ever sleepover. Honey, Mimosa, Sweetpea and Abigail had come over straight after school and were all staying the night. They had been planning and looking forward to the sleepover for weeks.

"My cousin Daisy and her friends have sleepovers all the time, although she has hers in the summer house, not in her bedroom," explained Poppy as she laid out everybody's sleeping bags neatly on the cushions Mum had put out for the girls to sleep on.

"Don't Daisy and her friends do lots of beauty treatments when they have sleepovers?" piped up Honey, who was quite a fan of Poppy's older cousin. "I wish we could do that."

"Well, actually, we can. Come and see," said Poppy excitedly. "I went to see Lily Ann Peach today at the Beehive Beauty Salon and she's given me all this

stuff. Look!"

"Wow! Make-up!" said Sweetpea. "My mum never lets me wear make-up. This is so cool. I love that bright red lipstick!"

"And sparkly eye shadow," gasped Abigail.

"Look at all the creams and lotions too!" said Honey as she examined the pretty bottles and jars. "Yippee!"

"I told you I'd sort it out, didn't I?" laughed Poppy.

"Ugh, what's that?" wondered Mimosa, pointing at a glass jar of what looked like guacamole. "Do we eat it with dipping chips?"

"No, silly," said Poppy knowledgably. "It's avocado face pack. Lily Ann said to spread it on our faces then wash it off after about half an hour."

"Cool . . . but what's it for?" asked Abigail.

"Um . . . it makes your face glow or something," muttered Poppy, who wasn't quite sure of the point of it herself but knew it seemed incredibly grown-up, if a little disgusting and slimy.

"Right," she continued, "I've made a plan for tonight. We can't waste a single nanosecond because this doesn't happen very often. Have you all brought the things we agreed on?"

Everybody nodded.

"OK then. Let's run through the list of what everyone should have with them," said Poppy, clutching her very efficient-looking clipboard.

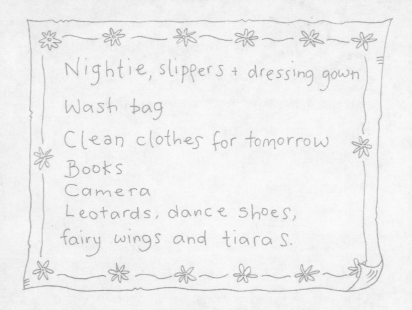

Nightie, slippers + dressing gown
Wash bag
Clean clothes for tomorrow
Books
Camera
Leotards, dance shoes,
fairy wings and tiaras.

All the friends rummaged about in their backpacks.

"Yes," they chorused. "Got everything."

"Good. So here's the plan. Let's start with the posters for cousin Daisy's band, the Beach Babes. Have you brought your art set, Honey?"

Honey produced a fabulous box of art materials which her mum and dad had given her on their last visit to Honeypot Hill, complete with several big sheets of

white paper, some stencils, stickers and a
calligraphy set.

"Check," she said.

"Good, that's the posters sorted then,"
continued Poppy. "After that we can start
the beauty treatments. I've got all that
stuff which we've just seen. Very well
done, Poppy Cotton, good job," she said,
patting herself on the back.

All the girls laughed. Poppy was great
fun, even if she *did* have a bit of a bossy
streak.

"After that, we need to practise our
dance routine for the Beach Babes' next

gig. Mimosa, did you bring your big sister's cool CDs?"

"Yep, here they are," replied Mimosa, and held up the bright pink CD player and karaoke machine she had brought with her as well.

"Excellent. After that it will be supper time. Yum-yum! Mum's cooked something 'sensible'. Have you got the goodies, Sweetpea?"

"Yes, I most certainly do!" said Sweetpea proudly, showing off a large bag of mixed sweets from the General Store. The girls were hardly ever allowed to eat sweets.

"Wow!" said Abigail. "I hope my dad doesn't find out!"

"And after supper, when Mum's tucked

us up in bed, it's officially 'Scary Story Time'. I've been to the library and got these!" announced Poppy.

The girls drew closer to examine the books Poppy was holding out: *Ghostly Galleons: Pirate and Mermaid Spirits*, plus *Highwaymen and Other Robbers*. And the worst ever was *Witches' Way*.

"Oooh, they all sound horrible," shuddered Honey. "My granny won't let me read *Witches' Way*. She says it'll give me bad dreams."

"Um, Honey," said Mimosa, "the whole point of a sleepover is to do things you *aren't* normally allowed to do!"

"I don't care what you say," said Honey, "I don't want to have nightmares. I'm going to stick with my *Care Fairies* magazine. You'll wish you'd done the same when you're too spooked to sleep!"

"Well, I think the creepy books sound

brilliant!" announced Sweetpea. "I'll read *The Highwayman* poem out loud. It'll totally freak you out."

"That takes us to 'The Witching Hour'," cackled Poppy, grabbing her Halloween hat from her dressing-up box. "Sleep if you dare!

"And in the morning," she continued, "my dad is going to take us on a nature walk in Wildspice Woods. He thinks we might even see some deer if we're lucky."

"Cool. I love the woods!" exclaimed Honey.

Chapter Two

The girls got to work on their posters,
and chatted and laughed their way
through the beauty treatments, which
made a terrible mess, then practised their
dance routines and songs. Later on
Poppy's mum brought them a delicious,
very healthy supper, which was balanced
out by Sweetpea's treats.

Poppy's parents did have to tick the
girls off a couple of times for making too
much noise and disturbing Poppy's baby

brother and sister, Angel and Archie, but apart from that they were allowed to do as they wished for the whole evening, which they all thought was utter bliss!

Once the girls had changed into their night clothes, they sat nibbling on fudge and sipping creamy hot chocolate while listening to spooky stories. Poppy had asked Mum if she could light scented candles, which Mum had agreed to as long as Dad lit them and blew them out. Honey and Abigail put on earphones and listened to CDs instead, flicking through their own non-spooky magazines.

"Time to settle down now, girls," said Mum as she popped her head round the door. "And don't forget to brush your teeth."

"Aww, ten more minutes, Mum," complained Poppy.

"Five!" Mum said firmly. "Then I'm

sending Dad in to put out the candles."

When the candles were out and the lights were off, none of the girls felt ready to go to sleep. They were having way too much fun and they didn't want the sleepover to end. Ever. So they carried on

whispering and giggling in the moonlight that shone through a chink in the curtains.

Suddenly Sweetpea sat up and pointed at the window. "Look out there. I think it's snowing. Wow!"

Poppy pulled the curtain right back to
get a better look. Sweetpea was right. The
garden of Honeysuckle Cottage was
covered with a thick layer of snow and
more was falling. The girls couldn't
believe their eyes. Surely it was much too
late in the year for snow.

"It's amazing," said Honey sleepily.

"Let's go out and dance in the snow,"
said Poppy. "We'll be the first people to
step in it. We can make a snow princess

16

with a tiara and beads and a feather
boa."

"But it'll be freezing out there," said
Abigail.

"Just layer up – I've got lots of hats and
scarves and socks. We can put our coats
on over our nighties. We won't be out for
long. Come on, it'll be fun," pleaded
Poppy.

The girls stirred from their lovely cosy
sleeping bags and flung on as many
warm things as they
could find in Poppy's
wardrobe. Then
they sneaked out
into the garden
as quietly as
possible so as
not to wake up
Poppy's mum and
dad or the twins.

"Let's be snow princesses!" said Poppy as she ran out into the fresh sparkly snow.

Soon the girls were rolling about making snow princess shapes and throwing snowballs at each other. Just as Poppy was forming the body of a snow princess, Mum stormed out into the garden in her dressing gown and slippers with a huge woolly scarf round her neck. She looked very cross.

"Poppy Cotton! What are you thinking of, bringing your friends out here in the freezing cold? You'll all catch chills. I'm responsible for everyone, you know. Your parents won't thank me if I send you home ill. Come on in, girls. I'll make some hot drinks to warm you up and sort out your hot-water bottles – then you *must* go to sleep. It's very late. Honestly, Poppy."

As the friends reluctantly trooped inside, they noticed that it was snowing even harder now. What luck! They couldn't wait until morning.

Chapter Three

The next day Mum came to shake the girls awake.

"Time to get up – breakfast's nearly ready!" she said as she pulled back the curtains. "Look, there's been even more snow!"

The girls looked sleepy at first, rubbing their eyes and scratching their heads, but as they began to focus, they all sat up and stared out of the window in disbelief. The snow was so deep that the whole garden was white and it was *still* snowing.

"It's as pretty as a picture, just like a Christmas card!" exclaimed Mimosa.

"It looks so fresh and clean!" said Sweetpea.

"It reminds me of whipped cream!" observed Abigail.

"I can't *wait* to go and play in it!" added Poppy.

"It does look lovely, I know," agreed Mum, "but it's so inconvenient. I was planning to go shopping today. Never mind, I expect it will stop soon. Now, why don't you all get washed and dressed and then come down to the dining room for a lovely big breakfast."

"Yippee!" cried Poppy.

The girls got ready as fast as they could, chatting and giggling as they did so. They were all very excited about going to Wildspice Woods in the snow

with Poppy's dad.

Mum put more logs on the dining-room fire and brought slices of hot buttered toast through, along with tumblers of freshly squeezed orange juice and steaming bowls of porridge. Dad appeared after a bit of a lie-in, looking very tired and dishevelled. He'd had a busy week at work, as usual.

"Morning, girls!" he said as he came and pinched a piece of toast from Poppy's plate. "I'm afraid we're not going to be able to go to the woods today. Ted, the postman, just rang. Apparently the snow is really deep and getting worse, so he's asked me and a few others to help him clear and grit the paths and doorways around the village – otherwise people will be stuck in their houses. This is the worst weather I've ever seen here. It could really bring things to a standstill. We'll do the walk another time – when this snow has thawed."

The girls were disappointed – they'd really been looking forward to their nature walk in the woods – but playing in the snow would be a good substitute.

"I think we should get you lot back to your own homes before the snow settles any deeper too," Dad continued. "You don't want to be stuck here for ever, now, do you?"

"We don't mind staying, Mr Cotton," chorused the girls. "We love it here."

"Well, that's very nice to know and we love having you, but I think your parents would probably like you back at some

point!" Poppy's dad smiled at them.

After breakfast Mimosa, Abigail and
Sweetpea went off to pack their things
and wrap up warm for the journey home
while Poppy and Honey helped Mum to
clear up. Honey didn't have to go home
because Granny Bumble worked at
Bumble Bee's Teashop on Saturdays so she
always spent the day with the Cottons.

While Poppy and Honey bustled
around the kitchen, making more mess

than they were clearing up, Dad turned
to Mum.

"Lavender, can you call the girls'
parents and tell them that we're on our
way? I think we'll go to Sweetpea's
cottage first, then Abigail's house, and
then I'll drop Mimosa off. After that I'll
go and help Ted and the others. Maybe
you should get Grandpa over here. You
know he never heats that house properly.
We don't want him to catch a chill. Not
at his age."

"James, there's no need to panic. It's just
a bit of snow. I know it's annoying but I
don't think it's a disaster! I'll make the
phone calls while you get wrapped up for
your great expedition. Me, Poppy, the
twins and Honey will pop over to see
Grandpa while you're out."

A few minutes later Dad emerged from
the cupboard under the stairs wrapped up

like an Inuit! He was wearing several
sweaters, a thick quilted jacket, woolly
gloves, a multi-coloured stripy scarf and a
long pompom hat with a furry trim.

Everyone laughed. Poppy's dad was making such a fuss about the snow while everyone else was just desperate to go out and play in it!

"I'm not sure if you'll be able to move in that lot!" said Mum, hiding a smile.

"Laugh all you like," said Dad. "I'm the one who's been listening to the news, not you. The Met Office is predicting that this will continue for days. You might all be glad of an outfit like this later!"

Mimosa had a fit of the giggles. "Mr Cotton, it's more like a bedcover than a jacket, and that hat is like Scrooge's nightcap!"

"Tee-hee-hee!" grumped Dad as he filled a backpack with supplies and went off to find a spade.

Mum made sure that all Poppy's friends were really cosy before they set off.

"Bye!" called Poppy. "Sorry the plans have all gone wrong. Hope you liked the sleepover!"

"It was really good fun, thanks!" called the girls as they disappeared into the bright white light. "Thank you for having us, Mrs Cotton."

Chapter Four

"Right," said Mum. "Shall we go over
and see Grandpa to make sure he's OK?"

"Yes please," said Poppy. "He can help
me and Honey make snow princesses in
the garden."

Poppy and Honey wrapped up in all
their warmest clothes. Honey had to
borrow some as all her really cosy things
were at home. Mum put on her winter
coat and a big fluffy hat — one of her
own creations — and then she dressed the

twins in adorable little all-in-one
snowsuits with matching moon boots.
They set off together towards Forget-Me-
Not Cottage, swinging the twins between
them since the snow was much too deep
for Angel and Archie to manage on their
own. Progress was slow, with the bitter
wind blowing against them and snow
falling faster and faster.

They pushed open the back door and
found Grandpa sitting at his kitchen table
reading the paper. He was wearing a
woolly jumper, a big scarf and his
famous fingerless gloves. He
turned down the radio.

"Hello!" he said
cheerfully, delighted
to see his family.

"Grandpa, it's
freezing in here!"
exclaimed Poppy.

"Aren't you cold?"

"Oh, I like to save my logs for when it's really bitter out," explained Grandpa.

Mum laughed. "Dad, I'd say today pretty well falls into that category. Anyway, we've got a lovely fire going at home and I've baked your favourite Victoria sponge. Why don't you come and stay with us until this snow thaws. James tells me that it could be like this for days."

"Oh, that would be lovely!" said Grandpa, who was always happy to spend time with his family, especially his grandchildren. "Thank you!"

"And Grandpa, will you help us make a snow princess in the garden?" asked Poppy.

"Of course I will. Just wait while I pack a bag and we can all head back together," he said. "A game of Operation by the fire might be in order too!"

After a tiring spell of snow-building
in the garden of Honeysuckle Cottage,
Grandpa left Poppy and Honey to it
and settled down in front of the fire in
the sitting room with a cup of tea and
a slice of cake.

"Dad, since you're going to be staying
with us for a few days, would you mind if
I borrowed a basket of logs from you?"
asked Mum. "I was expecting a delivery
today but I'm not sure it's going to make
it through in this snow and we're a bit
low."

"Of course you can, dear. Take as many as you like. I'll listen out for the twins for you," said Grandpa, settling even deeper into the big, comfortable armchair.

Mum came back from Forget-Me-Not Cottage with a fresh supply of logs and immediately set to stoking the fire. She hoped the twins would have a good long nap as she had a lot to do. As soon as she was happy that the fire was roaring she went upstairs to prepare Grandpa's room. Then she looked through the cupboards to see what she could make for lunch and supper. Luckily she found all sorts of things she'd forgotten all about. The cupboard wasn't nearly as bare as she'd thought. She made some lovely pea and ham soup for supper and an apple crumble too.

Just as she turned on the radio to listen

to the latest weather
report, the phone rang.
It was Granny Bumble.

"Oh, hello, dear."

"Hello," Mum replied.
"How's everything at the teashop?"

"It's very busy. All the people who are
helping clear the snow are popping in for
hot drinks and snacks. I've just seen your
James – absolutely frozen, he was. I gave
him a cup of tea and a toasted teacake
with butter and raspberry jam – that
warmed him up. He asked me to let you
know that he got the girls home safely
and that he's going to be a bit longer
than expected," explained Granny
Bumble. "Is everything
all right with you?"

"Well, the girls are
having a lovely time
playing in the snow,

the twins are asleep and Dad is snoozing by the fire, so yes, all's fine, except for this blasted weather. I want spring to come!" replied Mum.

"I've just heard the weather forecast and it looks like the snow is here to stay, for a few days at least," said Granny Bumble. "The only thing I'm a bit worried about is supplies. Aunt Marigold just rang from the General Store and she's nearly run out of bread, fruit and cheese. Everyone's panic buying because the newsreader on the morning programme told people to stock up. If Marigold's delivery van can't get to the village today, there'll be no more food for the rest of us. Same goes for my supplies. I can only bake if I've got the ingredients, and the road to Barley Farm seems to be blocked. It doesn't look like I'll be able to get anything today. I'm nearly out of

eggs too. But let's think positively, dear –
it can't go on for too long and I've
certainly survived a lot worse than this in
the past!"

"Yes, I suppose you're right," agreed
Mum. "It's really frustrating though.
Usually I just nip down the High Street
for everything I need, but I can't push the
buggy in this snow. Imagine living in this
sort of climate all the time!"

"Exactly! We only get this once in a
blue moon. I'll ask Marigold if she can
put aside some milk and bits and pieces
for you at the store, dear."

"Oh, thank you!" said Mum, beginning
to feel slightly concerned. "Bye for now."

An hour and a half later a very cold Dad arrived at the front door. When Poppy and Honey saw him come home, they decided it was about time they went in too. The snow was great fun, but it was also very, very cold. When they'd taken off their boots, they ran into the sitting room to warm themselves up and found Dad walking around like a robot, with

rigid arms and legs, pretending that he was frozen solid. The girls thought this was very funny indeed.

"I'd be even colder if it wasn't for this fabulous hat!" he said as he pulled off his Scrooge cap.

"I'm sorry we laughed at you this morning," said Mum, giving him a hug. "You were right, this snow *is* serious."

"Actually, I'm getting quite excited by it now," said Dad cheerfully. "It's an adventure!"

"What's going on in the village, James?" Grandpa asked, lowering his newspaper. "Nothing to worry about, I bet!"

"Well, yes and no, Grandpa," began Dad.

He went on to tell them all about the hungry birds who couldn't get worms from the frozen, snow-covered earth.

"OUT OF SUPPLIES"

DEEP SNOW AROUND...

Then he explained that many people,
especially the elderly, were starting to feel
the cold very badly. Like the Cottons, lots
of families had been expecting log
deliveries that day, but because of the
snow the log-man couldn't reach them.
Dad confirmed what Granny Bumble
had said about the panic-buying. The
shops were almost empty and there were
no fresh supplies anywhere. He also told
tales of frozen pipes and nasty accidents
on slippery paths.

Everyone looked at each other,
suddenly realizing that Dad hadn't been

over-reacting and that the snowstorm
wasn't all fun and games.

"Perhaps we should go down to Delphi
and Daniel's in Camomile Cove,"
suggested Mum. "They never get such bad
snow there."

"The roads are all blocked, darling,"
said Dad. "We're totally snowed in."

Chapter Five

Just then the phone rang again. It was
Aunt Marigold.

"Hello, Lavender. I've put by a bag of
groceries for you but there wasn't much
left, I'm afraid."

"Oh, thank you. You're a life saver!"
replied Mum. "They're not going to last
long though – my lot are a hungry
bunch. I don't know what we're going to
do if this weather lasts."

"Well, actually, I've had an idea," said

Aunt Marigold. "If everyone in the village shares out their food and logs, everything would go a lot further. We could make huge pots of soup and stew. We could play games to keep warm, pool our resources and generally keep spirits up."

"That's a brilliant idea," said Mum, suddenly feeling like a huge weight had been taken off her shoulders. "But where on earth is big enough for us all to gather in round here?"

"Cornsilk Castle?" suggested Aunt Marigold.

"Yes, I suppose so, but it's always so cold in there. Draughty too," said Mum. "None of the windows quite fit."

"Well, how about the Village Hall, or the Lavender Lake Dance School?" said Aunt Marigold.

"Hang on a minute," said Mum. She held her hand over the receiver and spoke to everyone in the room:

"We're trying to think of a place where everyone in the village could get together to share food and keep warm – any ideas?"

Grandpa drummed his fingers on the arm of his chair while he thought. "What about the Hedgerows Hotel?" he said. "It's always warm in there and they must have lots of supplies in their kitchens. They've got a generator too, which will be handy if the electricity lines go down. We could all pay our way in due course. The Woodchesters are very community spirited – I'm sure they won't mind."

Mum passed the suggestion on to Aunt Marigold.

"What a brainwave!" she declared. "I'll
call them right away! Bye for now."

Mum and Dad decided to pack a
couple of suitcases with clothes and
provisions for the whole family just in
case Aunt Marigold's plan came off. Then
they listened to the weather report on the
radio, which said that the whole region
was snowed in and that basic supplies
were in danger of running out.

Poppy and Honey sat in front of the
fire chatting.

"Isn't it exciting?" said Poppy.

"Well, kind of, but what if we do run

out of food or freeze to death?" asked
Honey.

"Don't be silly. It's an adventure, just
like Dad said. Anyway, Mum always has
loads of food in the house – which
reminds me, I'm starving. Mum, what's for
lunch?" called Poppy.

"I've made some sandwiches, darling,"
Mum replied.

Poppy rolled her eyes. She liked their
big cooked lunch on Saturdays: it was a
tradition. Sandwiches were strictly for
packed lunches and picnics – at least
that's what Poppy thought.

As the Cottons, Honey and Grandpa
munched on sandwiches, a phone call
came through from Ted to say that

everyone was indeed to meet at the Hedgerows Hotel at four o'clock.

"I've always wanted to stay overnight in Mimosa's hotel," exclaimed Poppy, delighted at the way things were panning out. "It'll be like another sleepover!"

After lunch Mum, Dad, Grandpa, Poppy, Honey and the twins finished packing their things, including all the food they could find in the house, loaded as much as possible onto a sledge, locked up and set off for the Hedgerows Hotel.

Progress was painfully slow. The twins were whimpering and the adults were struggling with all the things they had to carry. This was made worse when they ventured out into the deep snow, fighting against the biting wind and driving

blizzard. Then, just as they neared the Post Office, Honey tripped over something and fell awkwardly into a huge snowdrift, dropping all her bags as she fell.

"Ouch! My ankle!"

Chapter Six

Grandpa offered to take Archie while
Dad examined Honey's ankle. He realized
immediately that there was no way she
was going to be able to walk to the
Hedgerows Hotel. He would have to
carry her. He picked her up gently, being
careful not to knock her ankle, and
carried her like a baby.

"We'll have to load these cases and
Honey's bags onto the sledge," said Dad,
fearful of falling over while carrying her.

"Poppy, Grandpa, do you think you can manage with the extra weight?"

"I think so, Dad," replied Poppy bravely.

"We'll pull the sledge together, Princess Poppy," said Grandpa, smiling.

It seemed that nearly everybody in the village was making their way to the hotel, carrying bags and holdalls, plus boxes, crates and logs. And even though no one could travel quickly because they were so laden, there was a bit of a race to reach the hotel – everyone seemed to think there would be no provisions left for them if they didn't get there first! But it was impossible for Poppy and her family to rush.

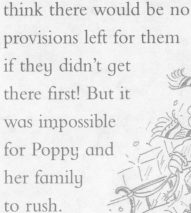

After what seemed like an eternity
they arrived at the Hedgerows Hotel,
to be met with the warmest of welcomes.
A huge open fire roared and crackled in
the hallway and a big tray of hot drinks
and shortbread had been placed on a
table next to it. Hotel staff were serving
the villagers and smiling warmly as
they went about their work. Even
Mimosa was helping to serve, very
proud that her family had come to
everyone's rescue.

Mimosa's mum, Mrs Woodchester,
was explaining to everyone what to do
next.

"When you've had a hot drink and a
snack, please take one of these forms, fill
it in and take it with you to the Grand
Ballroom," she said. "There, you will be
allocated a bedroom and a job for the
next few days."

FAMILY NAME: _ _ _ _ _ _ _ _ _ _ _ _ _

HOME ADDRESS: _ _ _ _ _ _ _ _ _ _ _ _ _

_ _

NUMBER IN FAMILY: _ _ _ _ _ _

AGES: _ _ _ _ _ _ _ _ _ _ _ _ _ _ _

SPECIAL REQUIREMENTS:

_ _ _ _ _ _ _ _ _ _ _ _ _ _ _ _ _ _ _ _

_ _ _ _ _ _ _ _ _ _ _ _ _ _ _ _ _ _ _ _

WHAT HAVE YOU BROUGHT

A) FOOD: _ _ _ _ _ _ _ _ _ _ _ _ _ _

B) BEDDING: _ _ _ _ _ _ _ _ _ _ _ _ _ _

C) GAMES / DVDS / EQUIPMENT:

_ _ _ _ _ _ _ _ _ _ _ _ _ _ _ _ _ _ _ _

D) LOGS: _ _ _ _ _ _ _ _ _ _ _ _ _ _ _

SPECIAL SKILLS: _ _ _ _ _ _ _ _ _ _ _ _

(EG. COOKING, SEWING, DIY, GAMES, ORGANIZER)

ANY ILLNESSES OR MEDICATION: _ _ _ _ _

OTHER INFORMATION: _ _ _ _ _ _ _ _ _

_ _ _ _ _ _ _ _ _ _ _ _ _ _ _ _ _ _ _ _

"Thank you!" said Mum.

"Before we do anything, we need to
attend to Honey," explained Dad. "She
fell and hurt her ankle on the way. It
may even be broken. Is Dr Latimer
here yet?"

Honey had been completely silent for
some time now and was being very brave,
but at the mention of the word 'broken'
she started whimpering. She didn't think
any part of her had ever actually been
broken before and it sounded very serious.
Poppy squeezed her friend's hand.

"Yes, he's in the ballroom already. You'll
find there's already a queue but Honey
must go to the front," said Mrs
Woodchester kindly.

Mimosa looked very concerned about
her friend and gave Honey a special
goody bag full of Hedgerows Hotel
postcards, pens and key-rings to cheer her

up. Honey tried to smile, grateful for her friend's sympathy, but she was in too much pain.

Mum quickly filled in the form and then caught up with Dad, Grandpa, Poppy, Honey and the twins as they

made their way down the long corridor
that led to the ballroom.

"Will Granny be there?" asked Honey,
through her discomfort.

"We'll find her soon," said Mum
confidently. "Don't worry, sweetheart."

Mum was concerned about Honey but
at least she didn't have to worry about
keeping everyone warm and fed any
more. The Woodchesters and their staff

were managing everything beautifully
and all the villagers were rallying
together.

Poppy couldn't believe her eyes when
she entered the ballroom. Almost everyone
she knew in the whole village was there,
including all her sleepover buddies. What
fun! Just then she noticed Granny Bumble
coming swiftly towards them looking very
worried indeed.

"Honey, love, what's happened?" she
asked.

"I . . . fell . . . over on . . . the way . . .
here," explained Honey in between sobs.
"It might even be . . . broken and it really,
really hurts."

"You poor darling," said Granny
Bumble as she stroked her
granddaughter's head. "We'd better let Dr
Latimer take a look. Poppy, be a dear and
go and get him, will you?"

All around the ballroom there were babies sleeping and playing, grannies and grandpas nattering, mums and dads catching up with friends, and children making up games and races. All the different generations were playing together and helping each other out. Lily Ann Peach had set up her beauty things on a table and was offering manicures and head massages for free! Madame Angelwing was instructing some girls – and boys – in ballet positions, and Saffron was repairing a split seam on a pair of trousers while her husband David had a look at a pet hamster that one of the village boys had brought with him to the hotel. Meanwhile someone else was setting up a microphone on the stage. Poppy was excited to find herself sharing this amazing adventure with so many of the other villagers.

When she returned with Dr Latimer, Honey was lying on a dining table with her foot all ready to be examined. Although Poppy was worried about her friend, she was dying to speak to Saffron and David so she left Honey, Granny Bumble and Dr Latimer to it.

"Our telephone and electricity lines were brought down by the heavy snow so we couldn't communicate with anyone," explained Saffron as she stitched away. "We just decided to get on the tractor and head up to the main village to get some supplies and see what was going on. Sally Meadowsweet came with us. But her mum and dad, Farmer and Mrs Meadowsweet, wouldn't come, poor old souls. They wanted to sit it out in their own house – they didn't want to leave the animals all alone. So, anyway, when we finally reached the General Store, Aunt

Marigold told us about her brilliant idea to meet here!"

"Actually, it was Grandpa's idea!" boasted Poppy, looking over at her grandfather, who was sitting in an armchair with a sleeping Angel on his lap, chatting to his old friend, Captain Forster. "Anyway, I must see if Honey is OK. She fell over on the way here and she can't even walk," she explained, enjoying the drama a little too much.

Honey was given a bandage, some pink pain-killing medicine and the Hedgerows Hotel wheelchair to get around in. Even though she now seemed much happier, Dr Latimer was keen to get her to the General Hospital at Camomile Cove as soon as possible as he suspected that she had a hairline fracture.

Chapter Seven

When all the villagers had gathered in the ballroom, Saffron's husband, David, helped Aunt Marigold onto the stage and then clambered up after her. He tapped the microphone and coughed to get everyone's attention.

"Ladies and gentleman, boys and girls! Welcome to the Hedgerows Hotel, where Mr and Mrs Woodchester have so kindly allowed us to seek refuge until the storm is over, the snow has thawed and we're

back in contact with the rest of the world.
A huge thank you to the Woodchesters!"

David paused and everybody roared
and cheered to show their appreciation.

"Aunt Marigold and Sally
Meadowsweet have looked through all
the forms you've filled in and have
decided on the following procedures:

"Since there are not quite enough
rooms to have one per family,
grandparents and extended family will
have to join them in the one room. Please
see the list on the notice board over there
to find out which room you will be in. We
will be serving three meals a day on a

relay basis. Babies will be given milk priority. Please don't store secret food in your rooms – we can only make this work if we all share everything. We will send out working parties each day to clear the streets and collect logs and other provisions. We'll pick up all stock from the Blossom Bakehouse and all vegetables stored in sheds and so on. If the snow lets up at all, we might venture to the coast on my tractor for supplies. But the forecast is grim. Please refer to the sheet pinned on the board to find out which job you've been assigned and report for duty after breakfast tomorrow. Many thanks for your co-operation. Feel free to go up to your rooms and settle in whenever you're ready."

It all seemed very well organized. Poppy thought that David was a real hero, running the whole rescue project, it seemed. Saffron looked very proud of him too.

When they checked the room list, they saw that Grandpa and the Cottons, plus Granny Bumble and Honey, would all share a large family room with its own bathroom and sitting room. They gathered their things together and made their way to the room. Poppy pushed Honey in the wheelchair.

"Wow!" exclaimed Poppy when she saw their rooms. "I've never slept in a hotel like this before. This is so cool. Look at the cute little soap bars and shampoo bottles. And the tea-making set. Bliss!"

When she had arranged all her things neatly by the bed that she was going to share with Honey, they decided to go exploring.

"This is like being on holiday." Poppy smiled. "Let's hope that the snow keeps on falling and the temperature stays below freezing. I want this adventure to last for ever – I wish you hadn't hurt your ankle though."

"Me too," agreed Honey, "but I really like my pink medicine and I wouldn't have had that if I hadn't fallen over!"

As they passed one of the rooms, they both noticed a huge box brimming over with fresh fruit, loaves of bread, boxes of cereals, chocolate

bars and cans of food. Poppy's jaw dropped.

"Secret food!" she whispered to Honey. "That's against the rules."

"I know," agreed Honey. "That is really mean and selfish. Whose room is it?"

Poppy tiptoed closer, peered in and saw Mr and Mrs Crowther, who ran the paddle steamer to Camomile Cove. Mr Crowther was munching on a banana and there was an empty chocolate wrapper on the bed next to him.

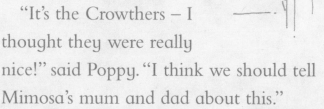

"It's the Crowthers – I thought they were really nice!" said Poppy. "I think we should tell Mimosa's mum and dad about this."

But as they were trying to decide what to do, they heard a loud gong. It was supper time already!

"Yippee! I bet this is just what it's like at boarding school," said Poppy, and she pushed Honey at great speed along the corridor and into the dining room.

Poppy had never enjoyed a meal so much – all the excitement

had given her quite an appetite. They had Aunt Marigold's tasty vegetable broth with crusty bread to start with, followed by fish, chips and peas and then pineapple upside-down pudding and custard. After supper Poppy pushed Honey back to their room very slowly – she was so full up she could hardly move.

The girls lay on their beds chatting and reading, and when it was bed time, they had a lovely deep sleep as new residents of the Hedgerows Hotel.

Chapter Eight

The next morning Poppy woke up before anyone else so she decided to make use of the amazingly luxurious bathroom. She ran a deep bath and poured in all the little sample bottles of bubbles and oil that she could find and splashed about happily. By the time she had finished, everyone else was awake and keen to use the bathroom before they went down to breakfast. While they did that, Poppy got dressed and they all went down to the dining room together.

It had snowed all night and she was
keen to go outside. While they were
eating the yummy food that had been
prepared by Granny Bumble and Mrs
Woodchester, Dad and some of the other
villagers were discussing what needed to
be done that day. It was decided that they
would split into two groups. David, Ted
and Mr Woodchester would go out on the
tractor to clear the road that led to the
main highway, and Dad and Mr Atkins,
the local builder, would take Mr Atkins's
digger and try to clear the
road between Honeypot
Hill and Camomile
Cove, via Barley
Farm, so that supplies
could get through.

"Can I come with
you, Dad?" asked

Poppy as she polished off a boiled egg with soldiers.

"It's going to be really cold *and* hard work," Dad replied. "I don't think you'll enjoy it."

Poppy's face fell. "Aww, please, Dad. I won't be any trouble. It'll be an adventure and I don't mind hard work," she said.

"All right then – as long as you promise not to whinge about being cold," said Dad.

Mum looked worried. "If you're taking Poppy with you, make sure you don't stay out too long – she feels the cold much more than you do, James."

Dad winked at Poppy. "We'll be fine, won't we? We're the rescue team!"

Dad was optimistic that they would soon return, laden with fresh provisions. Ideally he wanted to clear the road all the way to Camomile Cove, but at the very least he needed to get down to Barley Farm to collect bags of corn and also milk, cheese, eggs and butter for everyone in the hotel, and to check on the Meadowsweets. Their daughter, Sally, who ran the Lavender Lake Garden Centre, was very worried about her elderly parents out there on the farm with only the animals for company, especially since the phone and electricity lines were down.

"They should have come up here yesterday with me but they are very stubborn!" Sally explained to Dad. "Silly old doughnuts!"

"We'll try to persuade them to come back with us!" promised Dad.

"Thanks, James," said Sally. "They might listen to you!"

Poppy dashed off to her room to get ready to go out while Dad went to the kitchen to find some supplies for their journey.

"I'll meet you in the lobby in ten minutes," he called after her.

Poppy, Dad and Mr Atkins were wrapped up so well that only their eyes were visible, but at least they would be warm. They walked out to the car park, where Mr Atkins had left his digger.

When Poppy got outside she couldn't believe how much snow there was. It came up higher than her knees, and some of the drifts were taller than she was. Everything was so covered in snow and looked so different to normal that Poppy half expected to see polar bears and penguins roaming around the village!

"Wow!" she said when they reached the digger. "I've always wanted to ride in one of these. Now I'm part of the rescue team – I really am a rescue princess! Cool."

Mr Atkins climbed into the driving seat and started the engine while Dad lifted Poppy up into the cab, loaded up their supplies and equipment, then clambered in beside her.

The digger's progress was slow but steady and it had finally even stopped snowing. The three pioneers, Poppy, Dad and Mr Atkins, sang songs as they

ploughed their way through the deep snow. They were soon well on their way to Barley Farm.

"*The wheels on the digger go round and round, round and round, round and round . . .*" sang Poppy cheerfully as they bounced along, with Dad and Mr Atkins joining in for the chorus.

Then, all of a sudden, the digger juddered and spluttered and finally came to a halt, just over the bridge near the Village Hall.

"Oh no!" cried Mr Atkins. "This old thing never lets me down."

He turned the key in the ignition several times but the digger just coughed, so he got out and looked around the machine.

"Everything seems fine," he said. "I don't understand it – I've just had her serviced. Maybe it's the cold, but I'm sure

I put some anti-freeze in. I'll pop open
the bonnet."

Dad jumped
down too and
they both
peered at the
engine.

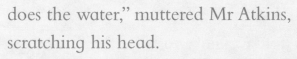

"Starter
motor's fine . . .
fan belt hasn't
snapped . . . oil
looks OK and so
does the water," muttered Mr Atkins,
scratching his head.

"What could it be then?" asked Dad,
who wasn't too sure about engines in
normal cars, never mind industrial
diggers.

Sitting in the cab of the digger all on
her own was boring and Poppy was
getting fed up. *Surely they'll fix it soon*, she

thought, *then we can be on our way. I was having such fun!*

"The only thing I can think of is that we've run out of fuel, James," admitted Mr Atkins when he could find nothing else wrong with his digger.

Dad's face crumpled. He hadn't thought to ask how much petrol they had. "Have you got any spare in the cab?" he asked.

"No, that I have not," said Mr Atkins, looking embarrassed. "This heavy work fairly sucks up the fuel. I'm sorry, folks. We're going to have to leave the digger here. They'll have some spare at Barley Farm – the tractors run on the same stuff."

Poppy thought this was a terrible situation. It had taken them ages to get this far in the digger, even though the distance they had covered wasn't that great. She was beginning to feel cold,

hungry and tired and she wished she'd
stayed at the hotel. Everyone back there
would be lovely and warm – they've
probably just had a yummy hot lunch.
And it had started snowing again!

"I don't think we have any choice,"
said Dad. "We're going to have to walk –
no one is going to come looking for us in
this weather. It's a long way back to the
hotel so we'll have to make our way to
Barley Farm and sit it out with the
Meadowsweets. If we can get some fuel
from them for the digger, Mr Atkins and I
can walk back, fill her up and then collect
you from the farm. How does that
sound?"

"Well, it sounds like a good solution to me, James," said Mr Atkins.

"But I don't want to walk," wailed Poppy miserably. "I'm freezing."

"Come on, sweetheart," said Dad. "You wanted to come and you promised not to whinge. It's an adventure and you'll warm up as soon as you start walking."

Dad caught Poppy as she jumped down from the cab. Through the blizzard, in the far distance, they could see the smoking chimneys of the farmhouse on Barley Farm. The three of them set off, using the smoke to guide them.

"How will Mum know where we are?" asked Poppy when they'd been walking for ten minutes or so. "Saffron said the phone lines are down on the farm."

Dad looked stumped. "Don't worry, Poppy, she'll know we're safe," he said, looking at Mr Atkins.

"Yes, I'd agree. She knows we're looking after you," said Mr Atkins. "And we'll soon be back at the hotel, safe and warm, hopefully with some supplies, before your mum even has time to worry, Princess Poppy."

"See, darling," said Dad reassuringly. "It's all going to be fine – we just need to keep walking."

"That's right. There's no point moaning at this stage. Let's make our way to the farmhouse. I'm starving too – the sooner we get there, the sooner we eat!" said Mr Atkins.

Chapter Nine

Meanwhile, back at the Hedgerows Hotel everyone was having a ball. Mr and Mrs Woodchester supervised everything and made sure that it was all running smoothly. Aunt Marigold had organized relay races, pass the parcel and quizzes too. Grandpa kept score and acted as the referee. Honey, Mimosa, Sweetpea and Abigail were playing cards, while some of the other children built snowmen in the hotel grounds. A group of adults were having a friendly argument about the rules of Monopoly, and those who had been assigned the task of cooking that day were busy in the kitchen making delicious cottage pies and various other tasty treats. Everyone was looking forward to hearing good news from the two scouting parties that had gone out earlier in the day.

"I do hope they manage to bring Mum and Dad back with them," said Sally Meadowsweet.

"I'm sure James will do his best," Mum assured her. "He can be very persuasive when he wants to be."

Their conversation was interrupted by Mrs Crowther bursting into the room.

"Dr Latimer, come quickly, please! It's my Ernest – he forgot to bring his medicine with him and he's having a bad turn. I've tried giving him as many sweet snacks as I can – that usually revives him – but it doesn't seem to be working."

Gosh, I'm glad we never did tell tales on them, thought Honey as she watched the drama unfold. *Poor Mr Crowther!*

Dr Latimer grabbed his medical bag and followed Mrs Crowther to her room. He was finding life very busy at the Hedgerows Hotel. He soon re-emerged with the good news that although he was keen to get Ernest checked out at the hospital as soon as possible, he was going to be fine; along with the babies and children, he was a food priority and must get exactly what he needed – little and often. The people working in the kitchen were beginning to realize that food supplies were fast running out.

By mid afternoon the team that had been clearing the snow on David's tractor had arrived back at the hotel with kindling and logs from Wildspice Woods as well as some food from the school kitchens and the café at the Lavender Lake Garden Centre.

"The digger seemed to be making good progress down towards the farm!" they reported to Mum, who was delighted to hear the news.

"They were certainly moving faster than we were!" said David. "I expect they'll be back soon, although they did have further to go."

When Dad, Poppy and Mr Atkins were still not back by tea time, Mum began to worry since it wouldn't be long before dark. She tried to keep busy but she was so anxious that she couldn't concentrate on anything, and in the end Grandpa had to feed and bath the twins for her. Every time Mum heard a noise she rushed to the lobby in the hope that it would be them, triumphantly returning with lots of fresh provisions. But it was always just the wind and snow battering the hotel.

"They only had one thermos of soup between them," said Mum. "The poor lambs will be absolutely ravenous."

"Don't worry, love," said Granny Bumble. "I'm sure they'll be fine. You know that James would never let anything happen to Poppy. She's got two big strong men to look after her."

"I know," replied Mum, "but I just don't understand why it's taking so long. They've been gone for hours and the weather's getting worse all the time."

"These jobs often take a lot longer than you expect. Perhaps they've been waylaid by an elderly person who needs their help, or maybe someone has made them a meal. There are still a few people in the village who decided to stay in their own homes, you know, dear."

"Of course, you're quite right," said Mum, in an effort to pull herself together. "They'll walk through that door at any minute."

Supper time passed and they still hadn't come back. Poor Mum couldn't eat a thing. When it was time for the children

to go to bed and there was still no sign of
Poppy, Dad and Mr Atkins, Mum couldn't
bear it any longer.

"We've got to do something!" she said.
"What if they're in trouble and need our
help? If they're outside, they won't last
long in this terrible weather. And look, the
snow is falling more heavily than ever."

"You're right, Lavender," replied David.
"This *is* serious – we're going to have to
send out a search party."

David organized everything very
quickly. Before long, a search party, which
included David, Ted, Mr Woodchester and

Hector Melody, was assembled. They
wrapped up warm, grabbed some torches,
spades, a tow-rope and a thermos of hot
tea and set off in the tractor towards the
farm and the coast, following the path
made by the digger.

The fresh snow meant that the tracks
the digger had made had almost
disappeared, so progress through the
village towards Barley Farm was slow.

"Well, the digger looks like it did OK

in the snow," said David, trying to
sound cheerful and keep everyone's
spirits up.

"Yeah, but why haven't they come
back yet if it was all going so well?"
wondered Ted out loud.

No one knew the answer to that and
they continued in silence.

"What's that!" said Mr Woodchester
as he saw something in the road in front
of them, lit up by the tractor's headlights.

"Looks like a massive snowdrift to
me," replied Hector Melody.

But as they got closer, they realized
that it couldn't possibly be a snowdrift
– it was simply too huge. David stopped
the tractor and they got out to have a
proper look. As they approached, they
all realized what it was at the same
moment: Mr Atkins's digger, almost
completely buried by snow.

They wiped the snow away and had a good look around the digger, calling out for Dad, Poppy and Mr Atkins as they did so.

"It just looks like it's been abandoned," said Ted, "and there is no sign of James, Poppy or Mr Atkins."

"They must have broken down," said David. "Maybe they decided to head for Barley Farm instead of turning back. It is closer, after all."

"You're probably right," replied Mr Woodchester, "but the road's completely blocked by the digger and the snow. We can't reach Barley Farm now."

"He's right," said Ted. "We'll never get past it. We'd better return to the hotel and report back. You can tell Lavender Cotton the news, David. I don't want to."

Chapter Ten

Poppy, Dad and Mr Atkins had found
it very hard going, trudging their way
towards the farm. Poppy felt as though
the deep white snow would go on for
ever, but just as dusk fell she heard the
familiar yapping of the farm dogs.
They were nearly there. At last! The
knowledge that they were so close to
the farmhouse gave Poppy a huge burst
of energy, and very soon they were
standing at the front door, stamping

their feet to keep warm and ringing the bell.

Mrs Meadowsweet came to the door wearing an apron over her dress.

"Hello! Come in, come in, you'll catch your death out there," she said as she ushered them into the big, cosy, candle-lit house. "What *are* you doing out in the dark in weather like this – and with Poppy?"

"You wouldn't believe what's happened to us," said Dad, "and how pleased we are to see you."

"Well, you can tell me all about it over supper – you've timed it perfectly." Mrs Meadowsweet smiled at them. "I've made a stew with dumplings and a rhubarb pie for pudding. There's far too much for the two of us. Take off those wet things and come and sit down."

Poppy ran in and flopped down in front

of the big open fire, delighted to be warm again.

They enjoyed a hearty and warming meal with Farmer and Mrs Meadowsweet in the cosy farm kitchen. The huge wood-burning stove was surrounded by puppies, kittens, hens and ducks. After the day she'd had, Poppy couldn't quite believe that she was safe now, but as soon as she'd had supper, she started to worry about Mum. She was desperate to speak to her and tell her that they were all OK. She knew what a worrier Mum was.

Dad tried to cheer her up but he was concerned too – he wanted to see his wife and the twins and to reassure Lavender that everything was all right.

Back at the hotel, the search party returned empty-handed. They shifted from one foot to the other as they worked up

the courage to tell Lavender what they had found.

Grandpa was waiting for them in the lobby. "Hello!" he cried. "You're back."

"Grandpa – bad news, I'm afraid. The thing is—" began David.

"Well, have you found them?" interrupted Grandpa.

"Not exactly, no. But we did find the digger! It seems they abandoned it – they must have broken down. All of a sudden their tracks just stop and there's just the digger blocking the road," said David.

"Where on earth could they be?" wondered Grandpa, searching for a logical explanation.

"We're pretty sure they'll be at the farmhouse or in one of the outbuildings on the way there," said Hector Melody.

Mum appeared at Grandpa's side.

She gathered that Dad, Poppy and Mr Atkins had still not been found and she began to panic. Everyone reassured her that there was nothing to worry about but she wouldn't listen. Her husband and her eldest daughter were missing. She couldn't just do nothing!

"I'm sure David's right and they've gone to Barley Farm. They're probably having a meal with the Meadowsweets as we speak, but let's call the emergency services, just for peace of mind," said Grandpa,  putting his arm around his daughter.

Ted dialled the number nervously and explained the situation.

"They're giving it priority because there's a child missing," he reported when he'd hung up the phone. "They're starting the search right away. Don't worry, Lavender, they'll find them."

Poppy's mum was beside herself with worry. " 'Missing' – that just makes it sound even more awful and serious," she said quietly. "Why did I let her go?"

Poppy was thoroughly enjoying herself at the farm and had almost forgotten about everyone back at the hotel. After supper Mrs Meadowsweet had run her a hot bath and now she was sitting by the kitchen fire wearing one of Mrs Meadowsweet's rather large frilly nighties. While the adults sat around the table chatting, Poppy concentrated on doing a jigsaw. Just as she was slotting the last piece into place, she heard an unfamiliar

and rather loud noise coming from
outside so she decided to go and
investigate . . .

Chapter Eleven

Circling above the farmhouse, fighting its way through the blizzard, with its floodlights shining down through the darkness, was a bright red emergency helicopter.

Poppy ran into the middle of the farmyard and waved up at the pilots, wondering who on earth they were looking for.

Perhaps Honey has got worse! she thought.

Then she noticed that the helicopter was looking for a place to land. The noise was deafening and the motion of the blades was blowing her around. Poppy ran inside again.

"Dad!" she cried. "Come quickly! There's a huge helicopter landing out here."

"Are you sure?" asked Dad, following his daughter outside to see someone getting out of the helicopter and coming towards him.

"We've had an SOS call," the man explained. "We heard that some people, including a little girl, were missing – in trouble in the snow. There's an abandoned digger up by the bridge but we haven't seen any people between here and there. We're looking for Poppy Cotton, James Cotton and a Mr Atkins."

"That's us!" called Dad.

Poppy looked confused. She had
thought that she and Dad were the rescue
heroes, yet now a rescue helicopter had
been sent for *them*!

"Climb in. We can take twelve at a
time. We've some people to take to
Camomile Cove General Hospital
after this. A Honey Bumble and a Mr
Crowther," the rescue man told them.
"So we've got to hurry."

"Honey's my best friend," said Poppy.
"Is she going to be all right?"

"We'll get her to hospital in no time
and then she'll be just fine," said the man
reassuringly.

"Just wait while we grab our things,"
said Dad. "Come on, Farmer
Meadowsweet, you and your wife should
come too. It's safe and warm at the hotel
and if I don't bring you back with me,

Sally will never forgive me! She's worried
about you both, out here on your own."

They could hardly hear each other,
the helicopter was so loud, but the
Meadowsweets nodded and went inside
for their things. They quickly laid out
food for their animals and packed up all
they could carry from their fridge and
larder.

"Be back in a day or two!" said Mrs
Meadowsweet to her pets.

"Wow, this is amazing!" said Poppy as she strapped herself into the helicopter and it lifted off into the air. "A true adventure!"

Just then, they all realized that she was still wearing Mrs Meadowsweet's nightie.

"Now who's wearing a silly outfit?" said Dad.

Everyone laughed.

What had taken Poppy, Dad and Mr Atkins almost a whole day took the helicopter a matter of minutes, and before long they were landing in the field next to Peppermint Pond and the Hedgerows Hotel.

Even though it was getting late and was still extremely cold, most of the villagers had come out, all wrapped up, to see it land. Mum was standing at the front of the crowd with tears streaming down her face. She watched as Poppy and

Dad climbed out of the helicopter.
Everyone cheered. Then they cheered
some more when they saw Mr Atkins and
Farmer Meadowsweet and his wife
emerge. But the biggest cheer was for all
the food they had brought from the farm!

Honey and Granny Bumble were helped into the helicopter, along with Mr and Mrs Crowther. They were all going to the hospital. Poppy waved at Honey, wished her luck, then rushed into Mum's arms, and Dad hugged them both. Mum held them really close.

"I've been so worried about you two – that is the last time I let you go on an adventure together!" she said, smiling, relieved to have them back in one piece.

As Poppy made her way towards the hotel, she noticed someone waiting for her by the main entrance. It was Grandpa. She slipped her hand into his and squeezed it. She saw him brush a tear from his eye.

"My rescue princess is back safe and sound – at last!" he said.

THE END

Turn over to read an extract from
the next Princess Poppy book,
The Fashion Princess . . .

Chapter One

Poppy looked through the aircraft window, desperate for her first peek of New York City. She could hardly believe what she saw, even though she had seen pictures in her guide book, the real thing was even more amazing. The needle-point skyscrapers looked like space rockets about to lift off, and there were masses of neon lights and thousands and thousands of cars driving through the busy streets in the early evening light. Everything looked twinkly. The view was completely alien to Poppy. She was used to the gentle rolling countryside around Honeypot Hill, where little cottages nestled cosily in the dales and the roads were almost empty of cars. She couldn't wait to explore the city!

Just then the captain announced that they should strap themselves in because the plane would be landing in ten minutes. As the plane descended, Poppy looked from her guide book to the window, trying to see whether she could spot some of the sights she had read about. What she really wanted to see was the Statue of Liberty. It looked so beautiful and she was fascinated by its history. Saffron had explained to her during the flight that the statue had been given to the Americans by the French in 1886 as a sign of friendship and to celebrate American independence.

As they waited to get off the plane, Poppy admired the outfits of all the beautiful and glamorous people filing past them along the aisle.

"Oh, look, Poppy. That's Tallulah Melage, the famous supermodel," whispered a star-struck Saffron, pointing to a tall, willowy girl with dark-blonde hair.

Tallulah was wearing a white raincoat tightly belted round her waist, with a hot pink scarf at her swan-like neck. Her long hair was tied in a loose ponytail and she had dark glasses propped up on her head.

Poppy gasped. "A *real* model! Wow! She's really, really beautiful."

"I know," agreed Saffron, "and she's so *incredibly* stylish too. I can't believe we've seen her up close rather than just in a magazine – she looks even better in real life!"

"We haven't even got off the plane yet and we've seen a real life supermodel," laughed Poppy. "This trip is going to be amazing. I'm going to have so many cool stories to tell Honey and the other girls at school."

"We're going to see a lot of beautiful people and exciting clothes over the next few days. It's going to be great," said Saffron, squeezing her little cousin's hand and leading her along the aisle. "Come on now. Time to taste the Big Apple!"

Poppy recognized the nickname for New York from her guide book. She smiled, grabbed her lilac backpack and followed Saffron.

Saffron had won
two tickets to New
York Spring Fashion
Week when her shop
was chosen by *Buttons and*
Bows magazine as the Best Clothes
Shop in the area. And because Poppy had
helped her win the prize by being so
helpful to the mystery shopper, who
actually turned out to be Bryony Snow,
the fashion journalist, Saffron decided to
take Poppy on the trip with her.

"I can't wait to see Bryony Snow
again!" said Poppy as they waited for
their bags to come round on the conveyor
belt. "I still can't believe she chose us as
the winners – especially me. After all, I
was only helping out in your shop for
the day!"

"I know, Poppy, but you made a very
good impression on Bryony," replied

Saffron. "It was mainly because of you that my little shop won."

Poppy smiled proudly as they collected their bags and placed them on a trolley. They breezed through passport control and customs and made their way towards the taxi rank. Their New York adventure was really beginning!